R0083738492

12/2015

 W9-BIP-909

A Beginning-to-Read Book

Dear Dragon Gets a Pet

by Margaret Hillert
Illustrated by Jack Pullan

NORWOOD HOUSE PRESS

DEAR CAREGIVER,

The *Beginning-to-Read* series is a carefully written collection of classic readers you may remember from your own childhood. Each book features text comprised of common sight words to provide your child ample practice reading the words that appear most frequently in written text. The many additional details in the pictures enhance the story and offer the opportunity for you to help your child expand oral language and develop comprehension.

Begin by reading the story to your child, followed by letting him or her read familiar words and soon your child will be able to read the story independently. At each step of the way, be sure to praise your reader's efforts to build his or her confidence as an independent reader. Discuss the pictures and encourage your child to make connections between the story and his or her own life. At the end of the story, you will find reading activities and a word list that will help your child practice and strengthen beginning reading skills.

Above all, the most important part of the reading experience is to have fun and enjoy it!

Shannon Cannon

Shannon Cannon, Ph.D.
Literacy Consultant

Norwood House Press • P.O. Box 316598 • Chicago, Illinois 60631
For more information about Norwood House Press please visit our website at
www.norwoodhousepress.com or call 866-565-2900.

LIBRARY OF CONGRESS CATALOGING-IN-PUBLICATION DATA
  Hillert, Margaret.
    Dear Dragon gets a pet / by Margaret Hillert ; illustrated by Jack Pullan.
      pages cm. -- (A Beginning-to-read book)
    Summary: "A boy and his pet dragon learn how to take care of their new pet. They learn to feed, walk, and play with their new dog. This title includes reading activities and a word list"-- Provided by publisher.
      ISBN 978-1-59953-706-1 (library edition : alk. paper) -- ISBN 978-1-60357-796-0 (ebook)
    [1. Pets--Fiction. 2. Dogs--Fiction. 3. Dragons--Fiction.] I. Pullan, Jack, illustrator. II. Title.
    PZ7.H558Ddt 2015
    [E]--dc23
                                        2014043662

275N—062015
Manufactured in the United States of America in Stevens Point, Wisconsin.

Father.
Can we get a pet?
My friend has two pets.

Maybe—
There is a place where they help
dogs and cats.

Ok!
Let's go take a look.

ANIMAL
RESCUE

Here we are.
This is it.

Oh, oh, oh!
So many dogs and cats.
Which one do we want?

Look at this one with the spots.
Here Spot, here Spot.

Oh, he likes me.
I want this one.
Can I have this one?

Yes.
He looks like a good one.

Come on Spot.
Come with me and Dragon.
You can be friends.
You will have a good home with us.

Here we go.
Away, away.
We will ride to my house.

We will stop here first for some dog food.
He will want something to eat.

This looks good.
He will like this.
Now we can go home.

Mother, Mother.
Look what we have.
This is Spot.

I see.
I see.
I will give him something to eat.

Now we have to take a walk.
Oh, here comes my friend.
He has a dog too.

Let's go over there.
They can play there.
They can run and jump.

They can play catch.

I have to go now.
My Mother wants me.
It is time for bed.

Come on Dragon.
Come on Spot.
It is time for bed.

Here you are with me.
And here I am with you.
Oh what a fun day, Dear Dragon.

The following activities support the findings of the National Reading Panel that determined the most effective components for reading instruction are: Phonemic Awareness, Phonics, Vocabulary, Fluency, and Text Comprehension.

Phonemic Awareness: The /p/ sound

Oddity Task: Say the /**p**/ sound for your child. Say the following words aloud. Ask your child to say the words that do not end with the /**p**/ sound in the following word groups:

pat, tap, mat	park, map, pack	set, pet, step
peach, reach, sleep	met, pet, up	spot, top, ten
seat, pea, keep	mark, pop, speck	sheep, day, page

Phonics: The letter Tt

1. Demonstrate how to form the letters **T** and **t** for your child.

2. Have your child practice writing **T** and **t** at least 3 times each.

3. Ask your child to point to the words in the book that have the letter **t** in them.

4. Write down the following words and ask your child to circle the letter **t** in each word:

not	get	too	want
pet	this	little	what
to	tail	that	spot

Vocabulary: Story-related Words

1. Write the following words on sticky note paper and point to them as you read them to your child:

    dogs   cats   catch   walk

2. Mix the words up. Say each word in random order and ask your child to point to the correct word as you say it.

3. Mix the words up again and ask your child to read as many as he or she can.

4. Ask your child to place the sticky notes on the correct page for each word, i.e. Catch goes on the page playing catch is talked about.

Fluency: Echo Reading

1. Reread the story to your child at least two more times while your child tracks the print by running a finger under the words as they are read. Ask your child to read the words he or she knows with you.

2. Reread the story taking turns, alternating readers between sentences or pages.

Text Comprehension: Discussion Time

1. Ask your child to retell the sequence of events in the story.

2. To check comprehension, ask your child the following questions:

    - How did Spot get his name?
    - What are important things you should get for a new pet dog?
    - What are some things they did at the dog park?
    - Do you have a pet? If so, what is it? If you don't have a pet, what kind of pet would you like?

WORD LIST

Dear Dragon Gets a Pet uses the 85 words listed below.
The **4** words bolded below serve as an introduction to new vocabulary, while the other 81 are pre-primer. You may wish to write the words on index cards and use them to help your child build automatic word recognition. Regular practice with these words will enhance your child's fluency in reading connected text.

a	Father	I	**pet(s)**	us
am	**first**	is	place	
and	food	it	play	walk
are	for			want(s)
at	friend(s)	jump	ride	we
away	fun		run	what
		let's		where
be	get	like(s)	see	which
bed	give	look(s)	so	will
	go		some	with
can	good	many	something	
catch		maybe	spot(s)	yes
cats	has	me	stop	you
come(s)	have	mother		
	he	my	take	
day	**help**		the	
dear	here	now	there	
do	him		they	
dog(s)	home	oh	this	
dragon	house	ok	time	
		on	to	
		one	too	
eat		over	**two**	

ABOUT THE AUTHOR Margaret Hillert has written over 80 books for children who are just learning to read. Her books have been translated into many different languages and over a million children throughout the world have read her books. She first started writing poetry as a child and has continued to write for children and adults throughout her life. A first grade teacher for 34 years, Margaret is now retired from teaching and lives in Michigan where she likes to write, take walks in the morning, and care for her three cats.

Photograph by Glenna Washburn

ABOUT THE ILLUSTRATOR A talented and creative illustrator, Jack Pullan, is a graduate of William Jewell College. He has also studied informally at Oxford University and the Kansas City Art Institute. He was mentored by the renowned watercolor artists, Jim Hamil and Bill Amend. Jack's work has graced the pages of many enjoyable children's books, various educational materials, cartoon strips, as well as many greeting cards. Jack currently resides in Kansas.